I0797541

INSIDE COLLEGE FOOTBALL

TENNESSEE VOLUNTEERS

BY TODD RYAN

SportsZone

An Imprint of Abdo Publishing
abdobooks.com

abdobooks.com

Published by Abdo Publishing, a division of ABDO, PO Box 398166, Minneapolis, Minnesota 55439.

Printed in the United States of America, North Mankato, Minnesota
022020
092020

Cover Photo: Mark Humphrey/AP Images
Interior Photos: Mark Humphrey/AP Images, 5, 7, 11, 28; Jack Smith/AP Images, 8; AP Images, 13, 15, 16, 19, 43; Kirk McKoy/AP Images, 23; Ed Reinke/AP Images, 25; Wade Payne/AP Images, 26, 36, 38; John Bazemore/AP Images, 31; Dave Martin/AP Images, 33; John Reed/AP Images, 35; David Stephenson/AP Images, 41

Editor: Patrick Donnelly
Series Designer: Nikki Nordby

Library of Congress Control Number: 2019954416

Publisher's Cataloging-in-Publication Data

Names: Ryan, Todd, author.
Title: Tennessee Volunteers / by Todd Ryan
Description: Minneapolis, Minnesota : Abdo Publishing, 2021 | Series: Inside college football | Includes online resources and index.
Identifiers: ISBN 9781532192494 (lib. bdg.) | ISBN 9781098210397 (ebook)
Subjects: LCSH: Tennessee Volunteers (Football team)--Juvenile literature. | Universities and colleges--Athletics--Juvenile literature. | American football--Juvenile literature. | College sports--United States--History--Juvenile literature.
Classification: DDC 796.33263--dc23

TABLE OF CONTENTS

CHAPTER 1

ROCKY TOP ON TOP

Quarterback Peyton Manning ended his storied college career with the Tennessee Volunteers in 1997. As a senior, he finished second in the voting for the Heisman Trophy. It is given to the nation's best college football player each season. During his three years as a starter, the Volunteers went 32–5. Tennessee was one of the premier college football programs in the country.

Many people expected the Volunteers—also known as the Vols—to take a step back in 1998. Manning had left for the National Football League (NFL). So had some of the team's other stars. Among them were defensive end Leonard Little, wide receiver Marcus Nash, and defensive back Terry Fair.

But Tennessee still had powerful and fast sophomore running back Jamal Lewis. Sophomores Travis Henry and Travis Stephens and senior Shawn Bryson were Lewis's top-notch backups.

Tennessee quarterback Tee Martin scores a touchdown against Alabama in 1998.

Tennessee also returned skilled wide receivers in senior Peerless Price and sophomore Cedrick Wilson.

On defense, ball-hawking sophomore safety Deon Grant was back. Also returning were junior lineman Shaun Ellis and senior linebacker Al Wilson—a tackling machine. The biggest question mark regarding ability centered on Tee Martin, the junior quarterback. But Martin would prove himself to be a winner as Tennessee put together a season to remember.

Tennessee began the year ranked tenth in the nation. Its first game was on the road against No. 17 Syracuse. The Orangemen had a star quarterback of their own in Donovan McNabb.

McNabb threw for 300 yards and two touchdowns in the game. Meanwhile, Martin at one point threw 10 straight incompletions. But Tennessee got a break late in the game. Syracuse cornerback Will Allen was called for pass interference on a fourth down. Then Tennessee senior Jeff Hall kicked a 27-yard field goal as the clock hit zero. Tennessee won 34–33.

TRAVIS HENRY

Tennessee faced a potential crisis when star running back Jamal Lewis injured his knee in the fourth game of the 1998 season. The team turned to two backups named Travis—Travis Henry and Travis Stephens. Stephens had trouble with fumbling. So Henry became the main runner, and he never stumbled. He rushed for 970 yards and scored seven touchdowns that season. "It was an opportunity to step up and show my talent," he said of Lewis's injury. "I prepared myself for a chance like that."

Tennessee offensive lineman Cosey Coleman (52) clears the way for running back Jamal Lewis against Georgia.

The schedule did not get any easier from there. Now ranked sixth in the nation, the Volunteers next faced rival Florida. The Gators had beaten the Volunteers five times in a row. They were also ranked No. 2 in the nation. Tennessee coach Phillip Fulmer called Florida "an all-star team."

The winning team, though, was Tennessee. And the biggest star was Al Wilson, the linebacker who chomped up the Gators. He forced

Tennessee wide receiver Peerless Price races for a 79-yard touchdown in the Fiesta Bowl following the 1998 season.

a fumble at the Volunteers' goal line. He also knocked the ball loose two other times. Wilson made tackles all over the field and kept the game close until Hall could make another game-winning field goal. This one was from 41 yards.

The 20–17 victory showed people that Tennessee had a defense that could handle anyone. If the offense could do its part, a national title appeared to be in reach. Fulmer's team then beat Houston,

Auburn, and seventh-ranked Georgia. The Volunteers allowed just 19 total points in those three games.

But injuries were hurting Tennessee. Lewis tore knee ligaments against Auburn. That ended his season. Al Wilson was playing banged up. But Fulmer had some solid backups. Many of them were sensational when they got their chance.

Henry took over for Lewis. He ended up running for 970 yards and scoring seven touchdowns on the season. Wilson remained the team's star linebacker. But junior Raynoch Thompson became a force at the position as well.

Tennessee continued to roll. Price returned a kickoff 100 yards for a touchdown against Alabama. That helped clinch a 35–18 victory. The win gave Tennessee its first 6–0 record in 29 years.

Then the Volunteers dismantled South Carolina on the road. A home

NEARLY HOG-TIED

Tennessee's perfect 1998 season was nearly ruined when No. 10 Arkansas Razorbacks came to Knoxville on November 14. Arkansas led 24–10 in the third quarter before Tee Martin ran for a touchdown and Jeff Hall kicked a field goal. A safety then cut the Arkansas lead to just 24–22.

The Razorbacks were still in control. That is, until quarterback Clint Stoerner stumbled and dropped the ball at his 43 with 1:43 to play in the fourth quarter. Tennessee recovered and then gave the ball to Travis Henry on five straight plays. His final run was the game-winning 1-yard dive with 28 seconds to go.

"Any game has an element of luck in it," Tennessee coach Phillip Fulmer said. "That's just part of the game."

win over Alabama-Birmingham moved the team to No. 1 in the nation. But then it stumbled. Tennessee fell behind by 18 points at home against tenth-ranked Arkansas. The Volunteers needed a miraculous comeback—and they got it. Tennessee recovered an Arkansas fumble with 1:43 left in the fourth quarter. Then Henry scored the game-winning touchdown with 28 seconds left. Tennessee won 28–24.

"If you're lucky and good, you've got a chance to be special, I guess," Fulmer said.

The Volunteers cruised through the rest of the regular season. Then they beat No. 23 Mississippi State 24–14 in the Southeastern Conference (SEC) Championship Game. The Vols were just one win away from clinching their first national title in 47 years.

Back in 1998, the College Football Playoff didn't exist. The Bowl Championship Series (BCS) helped determine a national champion. The BCS was a computerized ranking system designed to identify the best two teams in the country.

Those two teams then played a national championship game. Tennessee and second-ranked Florida State were selected for the Fiesta Bowl that January in Arizona. The winner would be the national champion.

Florida State was not a familiar opponent. The teams had last met in 1958. The 1998 Seminoles, meanwhile, were 11–1. They had speed everywhere and one of college football's most successful coaches in Bobby Bowden. But the Volunteers were not fazed.

Tennessee fans celebrate after the Volunteers beat Florida State in the Fiesta Bowl to win the 1998 national title.

Martin threw two touchdown passes, including a 79-yarder to Price. Tennessee took a 20–9 lead. Then Hall kicked a 23-yard field goal. The Seminoles scored a touchdown to cut the Tennessee lead to seven. The Volunteers marched back downfield. But Henry fumbled at the Florida State 10-yard line.

Tennessee needed a final defensive stand to hold onto that lead. And it made one. Grant tipped a long pass. Then cornerback Steve Johnson intercepted it. That sealed the Vols' 23–16 win and a 13–0 season—as well as a surprising national title the year after losing their iconic quarterback.

"I never came into the season thinking about replacing Peyton," Martin said. "We planned to come into the season and win games. We knew we could do it if we focused as a team. This is not surprising to us."

CHAPTER 2

GENERAL NEYLAND BUILDS THE VOLS

College football came to the Smoky Mountains of Tennessee in 1891. With students coaching, the University of Tennessee lost its first game 24–0 to a Tennessee college called Sewanee. Much about the sport—and the Volunteers—was different back then.

The team did not have a formal coach in any of its first five seasons. It went 12–11 during that time. The highlight was a 4–0 season in 1896. The school finally hired a coach in 1899. But none of the early coaches stayed around long. The team used 10 coaches to compile a 118–80–20 record in its early years. Then "The General" took over in 1926.

He wasn't quite a general then. Captain Robert Reese Neyland became an assistant coach at Tennessee in 1925. By the time his career was through, he was both a brigadier general in the US Army and one of the winningest coaches in college football.

Legendary Tennessee coach Robert Neyland had three coaching stints with the Volunteers between 1926 and 1952.

ROCKY TOP

"Rocky Top" is the unofficial fight song and anthem for Tennessee sports. Felice and Boudleaux Bryant wrote the song in 1967 in a hotel room in Gatlinburg, Tennessee, deep in the heart of the Great Smoky Mountains. School officials estimate the song is played more than 30 times per game on average.

On November 29, 1997, Tennessee quarterback Peyton Manning led the team past in-state rival Vanderbilt 17–10 in his final home game. Then he climbed a ladder in the end zone and led the band in playing "Rocky Top." The song's well-known chorus echoed throughout the stadium:

Rocky Top, you'll always be / Home sweet home to me / Good ol' Rocky Top / Rocky Top Tennessee, Rocky Top Tennessee!

Neyland replaced M. B. Banks as head coach in 1926. He brought a military way of doing things to the team. It showed in practice, in games, and in life. To Neyland, defense was the key to victory. Tennessee shut out 112 opponents in his 21 years as head coach. It also set a regular-season record by going 71 straight quarters in 1938 and 1939 without allowing a point.

The Volunteers ran the popular single-wing offense. In it, the ball could be snapped to any of three or four players in the backfield. Tennessee had joined the Southern Conference in 1921. The Volunteers shared the conference title in 1926, Neyland's second season. His teams lost just two games in his first seven seasons.

Neyland was building a powerhouse. Meanwhile, the university was expanding its home stadium. Shields-Watkins Field opened in

Tennessee coach Robert Neyland talks with team captain Ralph Hatley prior to a 1934 game in New York.

1921 with seating for 3,200. The stadium, which was renamed to honor Neyland in 1962, eventually became one of the biggest in the world. Today it seats more than 100,000 fans. As of 2019, its capacity of 102,455 was the fourth-largest of any stadium in the country.

After a one-year stint of military service, Neyland returned to the sidelines in 1936. Two years later the Vols posted their best record to date at 11–0. They scored 293 points and allowed just 16 that season. Tennessee also won the SEC and went to its first bowl game. The Volunteers blanked unbeaten, fourth-ranked Oklahoma 17–0 at the Orange Bowl. At the time, the national championship was decided by vote. Five voting organizations named Tennessee the national champion.

Tennessee's Hank Lauricella (27) races around Maryland defenders during the Sugar Bowl following the 1951 season.

Neyland's stars included senior linemen Bob Woodruff and Joe Little, sophomore guard Bob Suffridge, sophomore tailback George Cafego, and senior end and captain Bowden Wyatt. Cafego, Wyatt, and Suffridge were All-Americans that year.

The Volunteers were again unbeaten through the 1939 regular season. However, they lost to No. 3 Southern California (USC) in the Rose Bowl. It was the same thing the next year. Tennessee won all 10 games during the regular season. Then it lost to fifth-ranked Boston College in the Sugar Bowl. However, two organizations named Tennessee the 1940 national champion.

Then Neyland took another leave of absence. He was gone five years due to World War II. While he was gone,

SMOKEY

A blue tick coonhound named Smokey is the Volunteers' official mascot. A student poll in 1953 chose a dog to be the team's mascot. A halftime contest to select the dog was held when Tennessee played Mississippi State. The last dog introduced was one named Blue Smokey. He barked when his name was announced. Students cheered, and he barked again—several times. And Tennessee had its mascot.

John Barnhill guided the Volunteers to an impressive 32–5–2 record and two bowl games. In 1944 Tennessee won its first night game, beating Louisiana State (LSU) 13–0.

When Neyland came back in 1946, he predicted it would take five years "to put Tennessee back on top." He was spot on. The 1950 Volunteers went 11–1, and one organization named them national champions. But the team was even better the next year.

VOLUNTEERS

During the early 1800s, future President Andrew Jackson organized armies from Tennessee to fight in wars. Most members of those armies were volunteers. During the Mexican-American War, Tennessee Governor Aaron Brown asked for volunteers, hoping for 2,800. He got nearly 30,000. So Tennessee became known as the Volunteer State. The University of Tennessee's sports teams are named after this tradition of volunteerism.

The 1951 Volunteers featured guard John Michels and defensive tackle Doug Atkins, both juniors, and senior tailback Hank Lauricella. Behind them, Tennessee outscored opponents 373–88 and won all 10 of its regular-season games. Among those wins was Tennessee's first appearance on television in a 27–13 victory against Alabama. The Volunteers then fell to third-ranked Maryland 28–13 in the Sugar Bowl. However, the national champion was selected before the bowl games. And the choice was Tennessee.

Neyland stayed for one more season. He said goodbye before a Cotton Bowl loss to tenth-ranked Texas. It was the end of an era, but two new Tennessee football legends were on the way.

CHAPTER 3

MAJORS AND DICKEY

Two figures dominated the next 40 years on Rocky Top: Johnny Majors and Doug Dickey. Outside of Peyton Manning, many consider Majors to be the greatest player to ever put on a Volunteers uniform. In his first game in 1954, the sophomore tailback broke an 80-yard touchdown run in a 19–7 win over Mississippi State. It was a sign of things to come.

But that Tennessee team went just 4–6. Bowden Wyatt replaced head coach Harvey Robinson after that. Wyatt had been a College Football Hall of Fame player on Tennessee's undefeated 1938 squad. As the new coach, his main weapon the next two years was Majors. And in 1956, the Volunteers won the SEC title and finished the season ranked second overall.

Majors was the chief reason. Between rushing and passing, the senior accounted for 1,101 yards of total offense. It was his second

Tailback Johnny Majors was one of the best Volunteers ever.

straight year over 1,000 yards. He finished second to Notre Dame's Paul Hornung in the voting for the Heisman Trophy. The Volunteers went 10–0 before losing to No. 11 Baylor in the Sugar Bowl.

Wyatt stayed through 1962. He finished with a 49–29–4 record. But he didn't take the Volunteers to a bowl game after 1957. Wyatt was replaced by Jim McDonald, who lasted just one season. Then Dickey took over in Knoxville. He installed the "T" formation. In it, the quarterback takes all direct snaps, while tailbacks or fullbacks join him in the backfield.

Dickey opened up Tennessee's offense. He called more passing plays, recruited fast running backs and receivers, and also brought in strong linemen. One of those players was Richmond Flowers. He was originally recruited to run track in 1966, but he became a standout pass catcher.

Sophomore quarterback Dewey Warren led the 1965 team. Tennessee started the season 2–0–2, but then tragedy struck. Three assistant coaches were killed after a train hit their car. Dickey considered canceling the next game with Houston. However, it was decided that the game should go on as planned. The Volunteers won 17–8. They lost only one game that season. Then they beat Tulsa 27–6 in the Bluebonnet Bowl. It was their first bowl trip since 1957.

Then another tragedy hit the program. Linebacker Tom Fisher and tackle John Crumbacher died in a car crash in 1966. Again, the Volunteers responded. They went 8–3 and advanced to the Gator Bowl, where they beat Syracuse and its star running backs

Larry Csonka and Floyd Little, both future Pro Football Hall of Famers.

Dickey had turned Tennessee back into a winner. The team won all but its first and last games in 1967. Most polls had Tennessee ranked second in the nation. One named Tennessee the national champion.

The Volunteers were fun to watch. They featured stars such as center Bob Johnson, tight end Ken DeLong, and linebacker Steve Kiner. In 1968 Tennessee suited up sophomore receiver Lester McClain. He was the first black player to take the field for the Volunteers. That same year, artificial turf was installed at Neyland Stadium. The carpet helped the Volunteers play even faster.

THE DELONG BROTHERS

Brothers Steve and Ken DeLong were outstanding players for the Volunteers. Steve, a defensive lineman, won the 1964 Outland Trophy as the best interior lineman in college football and is a member of the College Football Hall of Fame. He was Tennessee's first national award winner. His son, Keith, played for Tennessee from 1985 to 1988 and was an All-American. Ken was a Volunteers tight end from 1967 to 1969, twice earning All-SEC honors.

Dickey coached at Tennessee through 1969. Then he left for Florida. Dickey posted a 46–15–4 record with five bowl appearances and two SEC titles at Tennessee. Bill Battle took over and became the first Division I head coach to win 11 games in his first season. The Volunteers finished the year ranked No. 4 in the country and defeated the Air Force Academy 34–13 in the Sugar Bowl.

Not much changed over the next two years, either. Battle's Volunteers went 10–2 and won bowl games both seasons. In 1972 sophomore Condredge Holloway became the first black quarterback to start in the SEC. His scrambling style was exciting to watch, and Tennessee soon became regularly featured in televised games.

Battle's teams eventually stopped contending for titles. He resigned after the 1976 season with a 59–22–2 record. Tennessee found an ideal replacement. Majors returned in 1977—this time to coach. He had just led Pittsburgh to the national title.

Majors knew Tennessee fans would have high expectations. One way he lived up to them was through recruiting. Among the stars

CONDREDGE HOLLOWAY

Condredge Holloway was the first black starting quarterback in the SEC. He played for the Volunteers from 1972 to 1974. He then went on to a 13-year career in the Canadian Football League. Holloway was such a good athlete that the Montreal Expos selected him in the Major League Baseball (MLB) draft. Even Tennessee basketball coach Ray Mears was interested in using Holloway as a guard.

In Holloway's three seasons as quarterback, the Volunteers went 25–9–2. As a junior, Holloway was named All-SEC. His motto: "No excuses, just play." Country music star Kenny Chesney was a 6-year-old Tennessee fan when Holloway was a senior. Chesney called Holloway his hero. Chesney later produced and narrated a film about Holloway called *The Color Orange: The Condredge Holloway Story*.

Tennessee coach Johnny Majors rides on his players' shoulders after a 1983 win over Maryland in the Citrus Bowl.

Majors brought to Tennessee were tight end Reggie Harper, tackles Tim Irwin and Bruce Wilkerson, receivers Willie Gault (a future Olympic athlete) and Tim McGee, defensive tackle Reggie White, and defensive back Dale Carter.

One of the most memorable seasons with Majors was in 1985. Tennessee beat top-ranked Auburn and its Heisman Trophy winner Bo Jackson that year. After winning the SEC title, the Volunteers moved on to the Sugar Bowl against second-ranked Miami. Miami wide receiver Michael Irvin scored an early touchdown. But eighth-ranked Tennessee put up 35 straight points to claim the win.

Majors left after the 1992 season, following 16 seasons in charge. His teams went 116–62–8, reached 12 bowl games, and won three SEC titles during that time. But another great player, and another national championship, were on the horizon.

CHAPTER 4

THE GREAT PEYTON

Phillip Fulmer spent 13 years as an assistant at Tennessee before taking over as head coach in 1992. His first priority was to find that one special player who could lift the Volunteers to the top. Fulmer found that player in Peyton Manning.

Manning's father, Archie, was one of college football's best quarterbacks when he played for Mississippi. Many people expected Peyton to follow in his father's footsteps and attend the school known as Ole Miss. But on January 25, 1994, Manning made a stunning announcement: he would play at Tennessee.

"I didn't want to go anywhere where I would be a star without doing anything," Peyton Manning said. "That's what would have happened at Ole Miss."

Manning would indeed earn his own accolades at Tennessee. The success did not come right away, though. As a freshman,

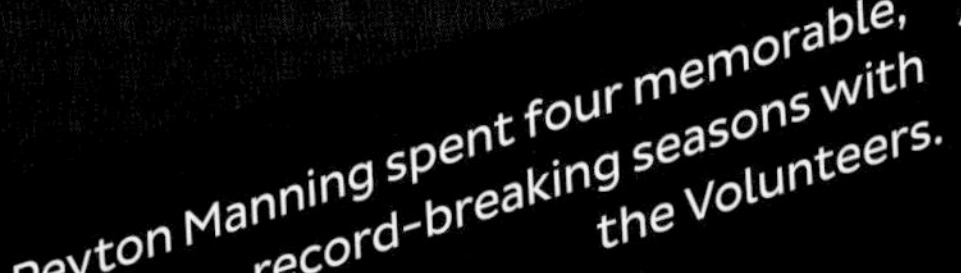

Peyton Manning spent four memorable, record-breaking seasons with the Volunteers.

Peyton Manning, *right*, starred in the SEC just like his father, Archie, *left*, but at a different school.

Manning was one of four quarterbacks at Tennessee. Senior Jerry Colquitt was the starter. Sophomore Todd Helton, a future MLB player, was second-string.

Colquitt hurt his knee in the first quarter of the opening game. So Fulmer sent in Helton. But the coach told Manning he would play at some point. And he did. Manning played for one series, on which Tennessee did not move the ball. Tennessee actually used one other quarterback in the game, too. But the thirteenth-ranked Volunteers lost to No. 14 University of California, Los Angeles (UCLA) 25–23.

Helton suffered a knee injury in the fourth game that season. So Manning was thrown into the lineup. He never sat down after that. Manning played well, completing 14 of 23 passes for 256 yards and two touchdowns, though the Vols lost at Mississippi State.

Manning went 7–1 as a starter the rest of the way and was named the SEC Freshman of the Year. Tennessee finished ranked No. 22 after knocking off No. 17 Virginia Tech in the Gator Bowl. But Manning wanted more out of his second season as a Volunteer.

Manning entered training camp as the starting quarterback. That helped him become a team leader. In 1995 Tennessee also began to

THE MANNINGS

Peyton Manning's father, Archie, was an All-America quarterback for Ole Miss from 1968 to 1970. He finished fourth in voting for the Heisman Trophy in 1969 and third in 1970. While Peyton was never known for his running abilities, Archie was a good runner as well as a strong passer. He was the second overall pick in the 1971 NFL Draft.

Peyton's younger brother, Eli, also went to Ole Miss. He finished third in voting for the Heisman Trophy in 2003. Eli threw for 10,119 yards, 81 touchdowns, and 35 interceptions during his time with the Rebels. Peyton's final numbers at Tennessee were 11,201 yards, 89 touchdowns, and 33 interceptions.

The San Diego Chargers selected Eli Manning with the first pick in the 2004 NFL Draft. However, they immediately traded him to the New York Giants. Like his brother, Eli Manning went on to win two Super Bowls during a long NFL career.

Manning takes the field during Senior Day in 1997.

pass even more—and win even more. But Fulmer had to suspend or bench 29 players that season for making phone calls with a stolen credit card. Manning was not involved. But it was a big blow to the Volunteers.

Tennessee needed to beat No. 4 Florida on September 16 to have a chance at the SEC championship. But the Volunteers could not pull it off. Even after building a 16-point lead, Tennessee lost 62–37.

Still, it would be a special season. The Volunteers went 11–1 and beat fourth-ranked Ohio State 20–14 in the Citrus Bowl. That gave

Tennessee a final ranking of No. 3 in the nation. Manning threw for 22 touchdowns, had just four interceptions, and set several school records.

The Volunteers were ranked second to start the 1996 season. Manning was expected to make the All-America team and to contend for the Heisman Trophy. The national title game would be the Sugar Bowl in his hometown of New Orleans.

Tennessee won its first two games. Then it faced Florida—and again lost. Manning had the worst game of his college career. He threw four interceptions as fourth-ranked Florida took a 35–0 lead. The Gators held off a wild comeback for a 35–29 win.

The disappointment carried into the next game. Tennessee lost to in-state rival Memphis for the first time. But the Volunteers still ended up 10–2 on the season and again won the Citrus Bowl. The team finished the season ranked ninth, and Manning was a third-team All-American.

By then, Manning had established himself as a top college quarterback. Now the question became whether or not he would leave Tennessee early to enter the NFL Draft. Most experts agreed he would be the first player selected if he left. Plus, Manning already had his degree. But he decided he was enjoying college life too much, so he stayed in Knoxville for his senior season.

As a senior, Manning passed for 3,819 yards and 36 touchdowns and was a first-team All-American. He called many of his own plays. Only a few college quarterbacks do that. He also posted better stats as a college player than his father, who was a Hall of Fame quarterback.

Many people think Manning was Tennessee's best player ever. But there was one big hole in his college career: Manning never beat Florida. He had his best game in four meetings with the Gators as a senior in 1997.

Manning completed 29 of 51 passes for 353 yards and three touchdowns. But Florida returned one of his two interceptions for a touchdown as No. 4 Tennessee dropped another one against third-ranked Florida.

But Tennessee bounced back. Manning led the Volunteers to eight straight wins and the SEC East title. They then faced No. 11 Auburn for the conference crown.

The Volunteers were trailing late in the game. But Manning hit senior wide receiver Marcus Nash for a game-winning 73-yard touchdown. As "Rocky Top" played throughout the Georgia Dome, Tennessee and Manning finally were SEC champions. "I will never forget how great that felt," Manning said.

HEISMAN RACE

Peyton Manning was the favorite to win the 1997 Heisman Trophy. But there was a lot of competition, especially from Michigan all-around standout Charles Woodson. Many were surprised when Woodson easily beat Manning for the Heisman. Manning said he was most disappointed because Tennessee fans could not celebrate their first Heisman winner. "I'd be less than honest if I said I didn't want to win it for them," he said. "I didn't know what to expect. I was excited just to be here as a candidate. I really had a lot of fun this year."

× Manning directs Tennessee's band as it plays "Rocky Top" following the 1997 SEC title game win over Auburn.

Even better, if third-ranked Tennessee could upset No. 2 Nebraska in the Orange Bowl, the Volunteers had a chance to own the national championship. But Nebraska was too strong. Manning's final college game was a 42–17 loss. In the spring of 1998, the Indianapolis Colts selected Manning first in the NFL Draft. And the Volunteers headed into a year of uncertainty.

CHAPTER 5

FINDING THE NEXT FULMER

Tennessee fans braced for a down year after Peyton Manning graduated. Instead, junior quarterback Tee Martin led the Volunteers to a 13–0 record and the school's sixth national championship.

Fans hoped that success would lead to more national titles in the following years. The Volunteers did indeed remain successful. But over the next 20 years, they only once came close to another national championship. When Phillip Fulmer left as coach in 2008, he said failing to win another national title was one of his biggest regrets.

The slide began right away in 1999. Fourth-ranked Florida snapped the Volunteers' 14-game winning streak in Week 2. The Gators won 23–21. Fulmer had begun to wonder if his team would ever stop being Gator bait. "They have beaten a lot of people,"

Quarterback Tee Martin plays bandleader after the Vols' victory in the 1998 SEC title game.

COACH FULMER

Other than Hall of Fame coach Robert Neyland, Phillip Fulmer was Tennessee's most successful sideline boss through 2019. In his 17 seasons as head coach, Fulmer was 152–52. The team went to 15 bowl games under Fulmer and won the 1998 national title. The Volunteers had a 67–11 record and an .859 winning percentage in his first seven seasons. However, they then went 85–41 (.675) in the next 10 seasons. They were 5–2 in bowls through 1998 and 3–5 after that. Fulmer returned to campus as the school's athletic director in 2017.

Fulmer said after dropping to 2–6 against Florida.

The Florida loss was one of three for the Volunteers that season. The third was a 31–21 defeat to Nebraska in the Fiesta Bowl. The Fiesta Bowl is a major bowl game, so it was not a bad season. But the 9–3 record was Tennessee's worst since Manning was a freshman.

Another Week 2 loss to Florida in 2000 got the Volunteers off in the wrong direction. They dropped three of their first five games. The team needed a spark to right the ship. And they got it from freshman quarterback Casey Clausen.

Clausen would earn the nickname of "Comeback Kid." His first college start came against Alabama. The Volunteers had won five in a row against the Crimson Tide heading into the game. Despite being sacked five times, Clausen threw two touchdown passes to senior receiver Cedrick Wilson. The Volunteers won 20–10.

There would be few comebacks and big wins the rest of Fulmer's time in Knoxville. Only in 2001 did the Volunteers come close to their

Tennessee quarterback Casey Clausen fights off a Maryland tackler during the 2002 Peach Bowl.

recent glory years. That year they went 11–2 and clinched the SEC East with a 34–32 victory at No. 2 Florida. A 45–17 win over Michigan in the Citrus Bowl left Tennessee ranked No. 4 in the nation.

While Clausen was a good player, he was no Manning. He ended up ranked second to Manning in school history with 34 career victories. Manning had 39. The Volunteers did have their share of standouts in the 2000s. Among them were tight end Jason Witten,

× Tennessee wide receiver James Banks reaches for a catch during a 2003 win over Fresno State.

wide receiver Robert Meacham, cornerback Jabari Greer, safety Eric Berry, defensive tackle John Henderson, and punter Dustin Colquitt. But none could lead the Volunteers back to the top.

Tennessee still had memorable games during that era. In 2003 the Volunteers beat Alabama 51–43 in five overtimes. It was the longest game in school history. Clausen starred, throwing for 283 yards and four touchdowns. He also sneaked into the end zone for a touchdown in overtime and then threw a two-point conversion pass to sophomore wide receiver James Banks for

Tennessee's final points. Two weeks later, the Volunteers stunned Miami 10–6, ending the Hurricanes' 26-game home winning streak.

Tennessee won 10 games in each of the 2003 and 2004 seasons. Then it fell on hard times in 2005. The Volunteers went just 5–6 and failed to play in a bowl game for the first time since 1988. There also were some off-field problems that forced the school to suspend and even dismiss players. But the team rebounded with two more strong seasons and trips to the Outback Bowl. However, Fulmer was fired after Tennessee finished 5–7 in 2008.

BATTLE AT BRISTOL

Few places in the world hold as many fans as Neyland Stadium. But Tennessee found one. It was Bristol Motor Speedway in Bristol, Tennessee. On September 10, 2016, the Vols played the Virginia Tech Hokies on a temporary field set up on the Bristol infield. A crowd of 156,990 fans packed the speedway's bleachers. That was a new record for college football. It smashed the old record by more than 40,000 people.

The Volunteers soon found out how hard it would be to replace Fulmer. Former Oakland Raiders head coach Lane Kiffin was the first one to try. Kiffin's dad, veteran NFL defensive assistant Monte Kiffin, served as the defensive coordinator. But Lane Kiffin stayed for just one season. He guided the Volunteers to a 7–6 record and lost to Virginia Tech 37–14 in the Chick-fil-A Bowl.

Lane Kiffin left for USC in 2010. Some considered him an up-and-coming young coach. But he made the most news for his

Tennessee wide receiver Vincent Dallas makes a catch during a 2011 game against Middle Tennessee State.

negative comments about other coaches and schools. Kiffin also got Tennessee in trouble with the National Collegiate Athletic Association (NCAA) for recruiting violations.

Derek Dooley was hired to replace Kiffin. He was the third head coach in as many years at Tennessee. Dooley's first squad was young, featuring 16 freshmen among its starters and key reserves. The Vols went just 6–7, losing the Music City Bowl to North Carolina 30–27.

The most notable game that season was a shocking 16–14 defeat at twelfth-ranked LSU. The Volunteers had too many players on the field for the final play. So even though Tennessee stopped LSU from scoring, the Tigers were given one more chance because of the Tennessee penalty. Stevan Ridley scored on a one-yard run, leaving many Tennessee players lying on the turf, crying.

Dooley's second season ended with a 10–7 loss to Kentucky. It ended a 26-game winning streak against the Wildcats. A 5–7 record also meant no bowl game, as the Volunteers finished last in the SEC East. The team went 5–7 again in 2012, and Dooley was fired.

ERIC BERRY

Eric Berry played at Tennessee from 2007 to 2009. He was one of the finest defensive players in Volunteers history. In the 2009 season he won the Jim Thorpe Award as the best defensive back in the country. He left Tennessee with the second-most career interception return yards in NCAA Division I history and was fifth in school history with 14 career interceptions. Berry became an All-Pro in the NFL, but he suffered several setbacks. He was sidelined in 2014, first by an arm injury and then by a cancer diagnosis, but he returned to become a full-time player again and was named Comeback Player of the Year in 2015. Achilles injuries caused him to miss almost all of 2017 and 2018, but Berry remained focused on a comeback.

In 2013 Butch Jones became the fourth Vols coach in six seasons. Jones came in with a strong resume from the University of Cincinnati, where he led the Bearcats to back-to-back conference titles. Jones said Tennessee was his "dream job." His enthusiasm got fans fired up for Tennessee football again.

Almost immediately, the Volunteers began playing respectable football. Their biggest victory came against No. 11 South Carolina on a last-second field goal. The next season, they were back in a bowl game. They made bowl appearances the next two years and ended the seasons ranked in the top 25. Jones developed some great players such as future NFL running back Alvin Kamara.

But by 2017, the good feelings had disappeared. Tennessee went 4–8 and 0–8 in SEC play, the first winless conference season in its history. The athletics department had seen enough. Jones was fired in mid-November, one day after losing to Missouri 50–17.

Maybe the best man to find Fulmer's replacement was the man himself. Fulmer returned to Rocky Top in December 2017 as the school's new athletics director. Within a few days, he had hired former Alabama defensive coordinator Jeremy Pruitt to replace Jones. Pruitt had led one of the best defenses in the country at Alabama. The Crimson Tide were in the top 10 in the nation against both the rush and the pass in 2017.

The Vols posted improved defensive numbers in 2018. Pruitt also brought in some great recruits. But on the field, they didn't improve much, finishing 5–7. Still, Volunteers fans hoped Pruitt would keep

Running back Alvin Kamara breaks out of the pack against Kentucky in 2015.

bringing in top players and keep improving the defense. With Fulmer watching over, they believed the program was in good hands once again. They were rewarded with a stronger showing in 2019, when the Vols went 7–5, and 5–3 in the SEC. All three conference losses came against teams ranked in the top 10. They capped the season with a 23–22 victory over Indiana in the Gator Bowl.

TIMELINE

1891

On November 21, Tennessee plays its first football game, losing to Sewanee 24–0 in Chattanooga, Tennessee.

1921

M. D. Banks becomes coach, and the Volunteers go 6–2–1 in their first season in the Southern Conference.

1925

Robert Reese Neyland is hired as an assistant coach. He takes over as head coach in 1926 when Banks resigns.

1933

Tennessee joins the SEC, where it develops great rivalries with Alabama, Florida, Georgia, Mississippi, Auburn, and LSU.

1938

Going 11–0, scoring 293 points, and allowing just 16 points, Tennessee wins the SEC and is declared national champion by five ranking groups.

1939

On January 2, the Volunteers beat Oklahoma 17–0 in their first bowl appearance at the Orange Bowl.

1941

Neyland leaves to serve in the US Army during World War II, and the Volunteers go 32–5–2 under John Barnhill through 1945.

1951

Tennessee takes the national championship by winning all 10 regular-season games. The October 20 win over Alabama is the Volunteers' first appearance on TV.

1956

Senior Johnny Majors finishes second in the Heisman Trophy voting as the Volunteers go 10–0 before losing to Baylor in the Sugar Bowl.

1962

Tennessee's home stadium is renamed in Neyland's honor.

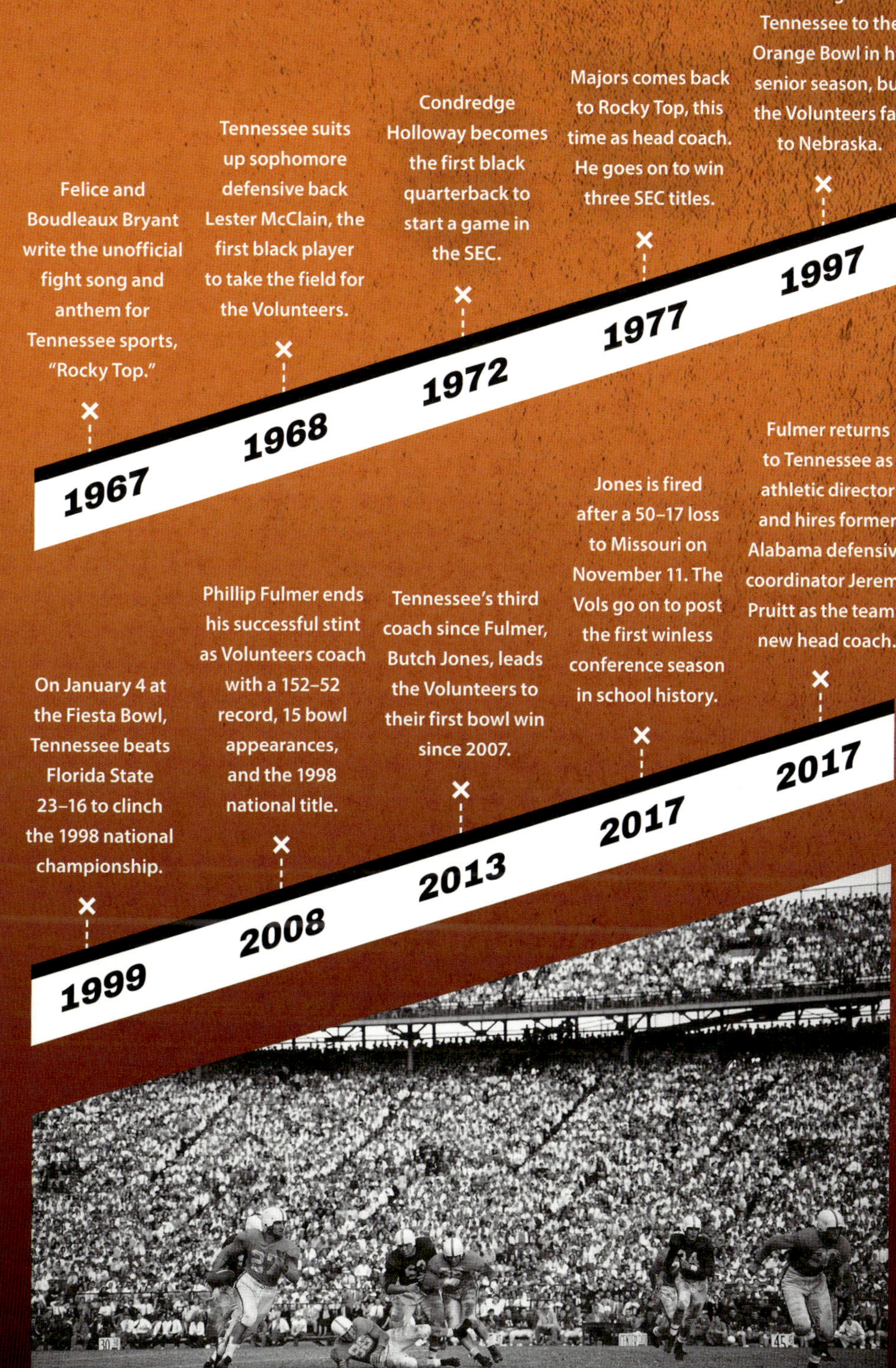

1967
Felice and Boudleaux Bryant write the unofficial fight song and anthem for Tennessee sports, "Rocky Top."

1968
Tennessee suits up sophomore defensive back Lester McClain, the first black player to take the field for the Volunteers.

1972
Condredge Holloway becomes the first black quarterback to start a game in the SEC.

1977
Majors comes back to Rocky Top, this time as head coach. He goes on to win three SEC titles.

1997
Manning leads Tennessee to the Orange Bowl in his senior season, but the Volunteers fall to Nebraska.

1999
On January 4 at the Fiesta Bowl, Tennessee beats Florida State 23–16 to clinch the 1998 national championship.

2008
Phillip Fulmer ends his successful stint as Volunteers coach with a 152–52 record, 15 bowl appearances, and the 1998 national title.

2013
Tennessee's third coach since Fulmer, Butch Jones, leads the Volunteers to their first bowl win since 2007.

2017
Jones is fired after a 50–17 loss to Missouri on November 11. The Vols go on to post the first winless conference season in school history.

2017
Fulmer returns to Tennessee as athletic director and hires former Alabama defensive coordinator Jeremy Pruitt as the team's new head coach.

QUICK STATS

PROGRAM INFO

University of Tennessee
Volunteers (1891–)

NATIONAL CHAMPIONSHIPS

1938*, 1940*, 1950*, 1951,
1967*, 1998

OTHER ACHIEVEMENTS

SEC championships (1933–): 13
Division titles (1992–): 6
Bowl record: 29–24

KEY COACHES

Phillip Fulmer (1992–2008)
152–52–0, 8–7 (bowl games)
Johnny Majors (1977–92)
116–62–8, 7–4 (bowl games)
Robert R. Neyland (1926–34, 1936–40, 1946–52)
173–31–12, 2–5 (bowl games)

KEY PLAYERS

Doug Atkins (DT, 1950–52)
Derek Barnett (DE, 2014–16)
Eric Berry (DB, 2007–09)
George Cafego (RB, 1937–39)
Dale Carter (DB, 1990–91)
Steve DeLong (G, 1962–64)
John Henderson (DL, 1999–2001)
Bob Johnson (C, 1965–67)
Alvin Kamara (RB, 2015–16)
Chip Kell (C, 1968–70)
Johnny Majors (RB, 1954–56)
Peyton Manning (QB, 1994–97)
Gene McEver (HB, 1928–29, 1931)
Carl Pickens (WR, 1989–91)
Larry Seivers (WR, 1974–76)
Bob Suffridge (G, 1938–40)
Reggie White (DL, 1980–83)
Al Wilson (LB, 1995–98)
Bowden Wyatt (E, 1936–38)

HOME STADIUM

Neyland Stadium (1921–)

*Denotes shared title
All statistics through 2019 season

QUOTES AND ANECDOTES

In 2010 school officials unveiled a statue of the Volunteers' great coach, General Robert Neyland, outside the stadium that bears his name. The statue is 9 feet (2.74 m) tall, weighs 1,500 pounds (680.4 kg), and was sculpted by Utah artist Blair Buswell. It shows Neyland kneeling.

"The way I look at it, it's kind of an honor to be able to graduate in three years. I feel I've earned the right to take my time, research it, and make the best decision possible."

—Peyton Manning in 1997 about deciding to play his fourth season at Tennessee rather than enter the NFL Draft

Today the Volunteers are known for their orange and white colors. A player from the first team, Charles Moore, picked those colors. He wanted them to match the American daisy—a flower that grew on campus. But those colors were not actually used in Tennessee's uniforms until 1922. The school debuted its orange and white uniforms in a season-opening 50–0 win over a Virginia college called Emory and Henry.

One of the most beloved sights on the Tennessee campus is "The Rock." A 97.5-ton chunk of Knox dolomite stone, the rock serves as a canvas for all sorts of messages related to Tennessee. Fans and artists use spray paint to leave their mark on the rock. Many of these messages have to do with athletics, including welcoming new football coach Jeremy Pruitt in 2017.

GLOSSARY

All-American
Designation for athletes chosen as the best college players in the country in a particular sport.

bowl game
A college football game played after the regular season, generally between two teams with winning records from different conferences.

conference
A group of schools that join together to create a league for their sports teams.

draft
A system that allows teams to acquire new players coming into a league.

legends
Players who are generally regarded as among the best to ever play.

ranking
A national position as determined by voters.

recruiting
Convincing a high school player to attend a certain college, usually to play sports.

rival
An opponent with whom a player or team has a fierce and ongoing competition.

upset
An unexpected victory by a supposedly weaker team or player.

MORE INFORMATION

BOOKS

Scheff, Matt. *Peyton Manning*. Minneapolis, MN: Abdo Publishing, 2016.

Wilner, Barry. *Story of the College Football National Championship Game*. Minneapolis, MN: Abdo Publishing, 2016.

York, Andy. *Ultimate College Football Road Trip*. Minneapolis, MN: Abdo Publishing, 2019.

ONLINE RESOURCES

To learn more about the Tennessee Volunteers, please visit **abdobooklinks.com** or scan this QR code. These links are routinely monitored and updated to provide the most current information available.

PLACES TO VISIT

College Football Hall of Fame
cfbhall.com

This hall of fame and museum in Atlanta, Georgia, highlights the greatest players and moments in the history of college football. Among the former Volunteers enshrined here are General Robert Neyland, Doug Atkins, Johnny Majors, Reggie White, and Bowden Wyatt.

Neyland Stadium
utsports.com/facilities/neyland-stadium/54

Neyland Stadium in Knoxville, Tennessee, has been the Volunteers' home stadium since 1921. With room for 102,455 fans, it is the fourth-largest stadium in the United States. Tours are available by appointment Monday through Thursday.

INDEX

ABOUT THE AUTHOR

Todd Ryan is a library assistant from the Upper Peninsula of Michigan. He lives near Houghton with his two cats, Izzo and Mooch.